# ANNA GROSSNICKLE HINES

# Don't Worry, I'll Find You

E. P. DUTTON • NEW YORK

for Jane,
who helped me go that incredible distance
from close to there

Copyright © 1986 by Anna Grossnickle Hines

LIBRARY OF CONGRESS CATALOGING IN PUBLICATION DATA

Hines, Anna Grossnickle.
  Don't worry, I'll find you.

  Summary: Sarah and her doll Abigail get separated
from her mother while shopping at the big mall.
  [1. Shopping centers—Fiction.   2. Dolls—Fiction.
3. Lost children—Fiction]   I. Title.
PZ7.H572Do   1985   [E]   85-16129
ISBN 0-525-44228-6

Published in the United States by E. P. Dutton,
2 Park Avenue, New York, N.Y. 10016

Published simultaneously in Canada by
Fitzhenry & Whiteside Limited, Toronto

Editor: Julie Amper      Designer: Riki Levinson

Printed in Hong Kong by South China Printing Co.
First Edition      W      10 9 8 7 6 5 4 3 2 1

One day Mama said, "Sarah, you
are outgrowing all your clothes. We'll go
shopping for some new ones today."

"At the big mall?" I asked. Mama
nodded. "Oh, goodie! I'll go get Abigail."

"I think you should leave Abigail home," Mama said. "We'll be very busy, and she might get lost."

"No, she won't. I'll take care of her,"
I said. "She really wants to go."

"Well, if you lose her, don't complain
to me about it," said Mama.

At the mall, I held Abigail tight. I held Mama's hand, too. The mall is a very big place.

"Now, if you get lost," Mama said,
"just stay put and don't worry, I'll find
you."

Mama took us into a store with clothes
everywhere. We found some just my size.

Abigail watched while I tried on the
clothes. I picked red jeans and a shirt with
a clown on the front.

At the next store, Mama bought me
new pajamas and some socks. I carried
the bag.

Then Mama looked for a blouse for
herself. She took a long time.

We took our packages to the car.

"Maybe we should leave Abigail here,
too," Mama said. "Aren't you tired of
carrying her?"

"No," I said. "I'm just tired of
shopping. And I'm hungry, too."

I had a hamburger and french fries for
lunch. Abigail just wanted one french fry.
Mama had a fish sandwich.

"Now the shoe store," she said.

I picked red sneakers, and Mama let me wear them.

"All we have to do now is find a present for Grandpa's birthday," said Mama.

We walked past a lot of stores. One had
suitcases, one had jewelry, one had records,
lots had clothes.

Then I saw one with toys in the
window. I saw a truck and a train and
a toy dog and a doll. Oh, no! Abigail!
I forgot Abigail!

Mama would be mad. Abigail would be
scared. I had to go back and get her!

I ran fast, past the record store and the
jewelry store and the suitcase store and all
the clothes stores.

I came to the shoe store. "Oh, good girl, Abigail! You stayed right where you were so I could find you." I gave her the biggest hug in the world.

We had to catch up with Mama. We hurried back to the toy store, but Mama wasn't there.

I had gone back for Abigail. Mama
would come back for me. We waited and
waited. Mama was taking a long time.

Maybe she was looking for me inside the store. Abigail and I went in to see. We saw games and toy cars and dolls, but not Mama.

I was going to show Abigail a backhoe,
but a lady picked her up.

"Why, that's my little girl's doll," a
voice said.

I knew that voice! "That's my doll!" I
shouted. "And my mama!"

"I'm terribly sorry," said the lady. "I thought she was lost."

"No," I said. "She wasn't lost. We were just staying put so Mama could find us."

Mama took my hand. "I was so worried," she said.

"It's a good thing I brought Abigail," I
said. "She helped you find me."

Mama gave us both the biggest hug in
the world. "It's a good thing," she said.